TIFFANY'S EMPOWERMENT

Shaneil McGawn-Francis

PUBLISHED BY:

Yah eh's
Anointed Publishing
Jamaica W.I.

DECLARATIONS FOR YOU!

I AM DESIGNED BY GOD FOR HIS PURPOSE.

I AM BORN TO WIN.

I AM NOT LIMITED BY NEGATIVE COMMENTS.

I AM DESTINED FOR GREATNESS.

I AM WHO GOD SAYS I AM.

MY FAILURES DO NOT HINDER ME; THEY HELP ME TO BE BETTER.

I AM A PRODUCT OF SUCCESS AND NOT FAILURE.

MY LIFE IS FOR GOD'S GLORY.

EXCELLENCE IS IMPRINTED ALL OVER ME.

I AM NOT WEAK; I AM STRONG BECAUSE OF GOD, WHO GIVES ME STRENGTH.

I AM NOT ORDINARY.

I AM A LEADER.

I AM THE HEAD AND NOT THE TAIL.

THE WORK OF MY HANDS IS BLESSED.

I AM NOT LIMITED BY CRITICISMS.

THE LORD IS WITH ME ALWAYS.

MY LIFE BELONGS TO THE MOST HIGH GOD.

JESUS LOVES ME.

I AM VICTORIOUS THROUGH JESUS CHRIST.

I AM GOOD ENOUGH.

I AM FEARFULLY AND WONDERFULLY MADE.

I AM GOD'S MASTERPIECE.

I HAVE THE MIND OF CHRIST.

I AM BRILLIANT.

I FEED MY MIND WITH POSITIVE THOUGHTS.

I LIVE MY LIFE ACCORDING TO GOD'S AGENDA.

The day Tiffany had been waiting for had finally come, but she couldn't seem to find the courage to leave her bathroom. With much nervousness, she stared at her reflection in the mirror. As the seconds ticked away, so did her conscious gaze, and soon she was deep in thought. She wondered how she had gotten here and how she had been chosen to be the speaker of the Female Empowerment Day at her primary school. After all, people never failed to tell her she was never and would never be good enough.

As Tiffany looked at herself in the mirror, she recalled the days when even she doubted who she was. She could remember being a strong-willed girl who knew exactly what she wanted, but her peers, people in her community, and even a few of her teachers doubted her potential. Nevertheless, she pushed ahead, and here she was about to speak to girls whom she was just a little older than. Tiffany was so deep in thought as she reflected on the negative things that people had said about her that she didn't even hear her little sister calling.

The little voice interrupted her deep thoughts with a great shriek.

"Tiff! Tiffany!" Tiffany was hurled back to

reality as the little voice echoed through the bathroom walls.

*"**Yes, Bre**,"* she replied amusingly.

*"**Mom is asking that you come down for breakfast now**,"* Bre transitioned to her soft, little-sister tone.

Bre admired and adored her big sister very much. Although Tiffany was sometimes annoyed at how clingy her sister got, she was happy she had a little sister. Bre thought so much of Tiffany and wanted desperately to be like her. As Tiffany opened the bathroom door, Bre looked at her with a warm smile, stretched forth her hand, and ushered her proudly in the direction of the kitchen.

Tiffany returned the warm smile and touched Bre on the head as she walked by her. Even though she got on her nerves so much, she still loved her baby sister.

Tiffany's eyes sparkled, and her taste buds danced in anticipation as she walked into the kitchen to see a wonderfully made breakfast laid on the table. Tiffany's mom didn't have much, but as a single parent, she worked hard to ensure that her two girls got what they needed.

"Tiffany?" her mom enquired softly. *"Are you ok? You were in the bathroom for quite some time."*

"I am ok, mom. I am just a bit nervous about today. That's all," muttered Tiffany with

her head hung.

"*There is nothing wrong with being nervous, Tiffany. You have been working on your speech for the function for a while now, and it is wonderful,*" her mom reassured. "**You have written from your heart, and that will be good enough to connect with the girls you will be talking to today. It doesn't matter what people have said about you in the past, Tiffany. You have the ability to change that, and you have been given this opportunity to empower others. So, stand firm with your head held high and do what you have been asked to do with much pride and dignity.**"

Tiffany's mom, Brenda, gave her a warm smile and a kiss on her forehead. Brenda believed in her daughters' abilities and often fueled them with encouragement every chance she got. She believed in growing her princesses on the basis of love despite the fact that she was not financially secure.

"You always have the right things to say, Mom," Tiffany responded with a smile as she looked straight into her mother's loving and reassuring eyes.

Overhearing their discussion, Bre admiringly

walked over to her role model and big sister and

hugged her tightly.

"You are already my hero and will always be my hero, no matter what," Bre chimed in with a gleeful, enthusiastic grin.

At the sight of her two daughters displaying the strong family values of love and support that she had engendered, Brenda proudly walked over to them and gave them both a big hug. As they cuddled, the kitchen went silent for a minute, but love and togetherness shouted ecstatically. In her heart and with renewed confidence, Tiffany said, **"I know I can do it, and I will."**

The time had fast approached, and Tiffany was making her final preparations. She was still a little nervous, but it was nothing she couldn't handle. A smile widened across her face as she recalled the kitchen encounter earlier in the day.

As Tiffany walked through the school's auditorium, she greeted and spoke with some of her former teachers. It had been seven years since she graduated from the school so quite a few people still remembered her. Tiffany graduated from high school as the valedictorian and acquired a full scholarship to study law at one of the top universities in her country. Due to her extensive contribution to her school and community mentorship programs and her voluntary involvement, she received awards at the school and community levels.

The auditorium did not change much. The big ceiling fans still hung, making much effort to cool the big blue and white room. Her vision caught the beautifully decorated podium at the center of the stage. With the detailed eye of a strategic interior decorator, the green plants were intentionally placed at each corner of the stage and throughout the room. The two speaker boxes were placed on either side of the stage facing the auditorium. The room was filled with sounds of chatter as some students were busy talking to their friends. Others moved about in their seats, while some looked restless as though that was the last place they wanted to be. As Tiffany gazed into the huge

group of female students of varying ages, it was

as though she could see herself seated in front

of her, shyly trying to make eye contact. She was a very quiet student, and during assemblies like these, she was always somewhere in the middle, trying to get a glimpse of what was happening up front.

Floods of memories rushed through her mind, and she drifted off into deep thought again. She could see the lips of the students moving, but the room was so quiet to her. Her thoughts were filled with recollections of happenings that occurred when she was a student at that very school.

"Excuse me. Excuse me," a very sweet voice uttered. ***"Are you Tiffany James?"***

Tiffany looked down from the platform to see this cute little face staring up at her.

*"**Yes, I am**,"* Tiffany replied with a smile.

*"**I heard that a past student was coming to speak today, but I was expecting you to be much bigger**,"* she said sweetly.

Tiffany smiled amusingly.

Like a militant colonel, the principal approached the platform, and instantaneously, the entire room went silent. By the time Tiffany looked back down to address the little girl, she had already walked back to her seat.

The ceremony began with devotion,

welcome, greetings, and performances from the students. Tiffany nervously looked down at her program and realized that she was next.

Throughout her introduction, the room went silent, and occasionally, students stared at her. At the sound of applause, Tiffany walked to the podium. As she gave her initial remarks, she froze for what seemed to be a minute. But that freeze thawed quickly.

She began to speak.

"Many of you may be wondering: what

is it that this little girl could possibly have to say to us today. She looks almost as tiny as we do."

The crowd chuckled. She continued.

"Let me see by the raising of hands all those persons who were told by others that they will never amount to anything."

A few students, including teachers, raised their hands, some confidently and others reluctantly.

"Raise your hands if you believe you will not succeed."

The room went silent, and the girls looked

around at each other, but no one raised her hand.

"I am sure that at the first glance at me, you may have wondered what I will be talking to you about. You may have whispered to a friend, 'She is just a young girl.' Yes, I am a young girl, but I, too, like many of you, was put down by the mouths of others in my younger years. I was told I would not succeed because I wasn't the most brilliant child. At first, I believed them, and I avoided anything and everything that would uplift me. But then I realized that no one should have that authority to determine who I

would be and what I would become. Today, I come to tell you that you all have a purpose in this life. You are destined for greatness. You may doubtfully wonder, 'Who me? Greatness?' Yes, you! What people say to us can do one of two things: make or break us. You decide what it is you want. You can use negativity as a ladder of motivation to climb further; ultimately, the negativity spoken will be proven wrong. There are persons who may bully you and make you feel less than who you are, but think about it. If someone bullies you, does it mean that you are weak and they are strong?

Absolutely not! Bullies go through their heartaches and pains of life for whatever reason, and they just search for persons to pour on their frustration. Some of your schoolmates may call you names and say cruel things about you. But should you believe them? Again, I say no. It will hurt to hear people say awful things about you because we are human beings, but what do you do when those things are said?

Remember that it will only hurt you if you start to believe them. If you know you are a brilliant girl, you are beautiful, and you are talented, why should you allow the negativity to affect you to the point where you stop thinking highly of yourself? Come on, girls. Be stronger than what people make you out to be. Imagine if females uplifted themselves and took their rightful places in society. How powerful you would be! Rise up, children of the most high God. Soar above criticism. Soar above negativity and rise above defeat."

Tiffany took a moment to look at the young girls in front of her, who were undistractedly latching onto every word that was uttered. Continuously, the girls clapped or nodded in agreement with what she was saying.

Unexpectedly, even to herself, Tiffany walked to the front of the podium and sat on the floor. She had even forgotten about the script she

spent so much time preparing. This was the decisive moment when she would speak from her heart to their heart. She flashed her eyes across the room and continued.

"I have always wanted to do my best at everything I did. Despite this, I often doubted my true abilities, which were embedded inside of me. I realized that not until I believed I could t I actually started to achieve my goals. The doubt has not taken me anywhere but down a road potholed with fear, fear of failing. This negative thinking led me to doubt if I should even begin. You see, girls, fear kills dreams and potential. If you haven't tried, do you think you will know the end result? Many of you may be intimidated by your peers because they are

scoring more than you are. You may get discouraged and think you are not good enough. Today, I say to you, don't compare yourselves to others or measure your success based on someone else's outcome. Do you think I was a top student in primary school? Actually, I was far from that. My teachers can tell you."

Tiffany, looking in the direction of the teachers, pointed at them and smiled. The girls followed her gaze and quickly refocused their eyes to the platform where she was.

Tiffany continued.

"I actually struggled, but do you know why I am here today, sitting in front of you? I was determined and motivated to achieve my goals. I discovered that I had the power through God to overcome the odds, the criticisms, and the greatest challenge – ourselves."

Tiffany paused and asked, ***"How many of you have ever told yourself that you couldn't do something when you never even tried? Oftentimes, we are the ones to put a limit on our abilities. We must learn to encourage ourselves by believing that 'Greater is He who is in [us] than he that is in the world.'***

God does not see us as the world sees us or as we see the world. God has not placed a limit on us, so why should we? There is nothing impossible for you to do. Possibilities lie within you. You are born and destined for greatness. But trust me, girls; you will not see that greatness even if it stares you in the face if you are constantly dwelling on the lies that people try to force down your throats: the lies that you will not be successful, the lies that you are ugly, you are no good, you are dull, you are stupid. Who on this earth has the ability to determine who the Creator above created you to be? Think about it for a moment – no one.

People will speak negatively about you, yes, because they have freedom of speech. But why should their negative words affect you? The girl seated in front of you today was never this positive. In fact, in retrospect, I had to rise above all the negativity that I heard throughout the course of my life.

I had to rise, take a stance, and bellow convincingly to myself, 'This ends now. I am taking back my destiny from those who spoke against me. I am what God wants and has made me to be. I am great. I am a leader. I am strong. I am destined for greatness, and

I am a child of the Most High God.'"

Cheers and applause rang out in the auditorium as all the girls stood clapping and cheering Tiffany enthusiastically.

As they retook their seats, Tiffany continued.

"Let me see the hands of those who believe that greatness is inside of you."

All the hands were hoisted in the auditorium ecstatically.

"Ladies, you may leave here today believing that greatness is in you, and someone says something negative to you, and all of a sudden, you forget what you believed. We are human beings, and we may be affected by what people say. But you have to take a stand. Say enough is enough. Take back your God-given power of authority over who you are. People will say harsh things to you, but you choose what you want to

believe, and what you believe affects you. So, as we leave here today, ask yourselves, 'What will I believe today and henceforth?' Remember that greater is He who is in you than he who is in the world.

Believe in your predestined gifts.

Believe in YOU and most importantly, believe in God who created YOU to be greatly great."

The girls all stood and cheered as Tiffany walked back confidently to her seat.

"I did it," she thought as she looked at the girls, still clapping and cheering.

She gazed right into the face of the little girl who had spoken to her earlier, and her little face was beaming as her lips widened with a bright smile. She nodded at her, and Tiffany waved. It was as though she was saying, ***"You are small, but you spoke well."***

Tiffany was pleased with herself, and as she left the auditorium that day, she reflected on everything she had said. She, too, had embedded all her very own words deep inside her because she, too, was **DESTINED FOR GREATNESS.**

I am Destined for Greatness.

Write your Affirmations/Declarations below:
(Feed your mind with positive thoughts)